NEGATIVE cat

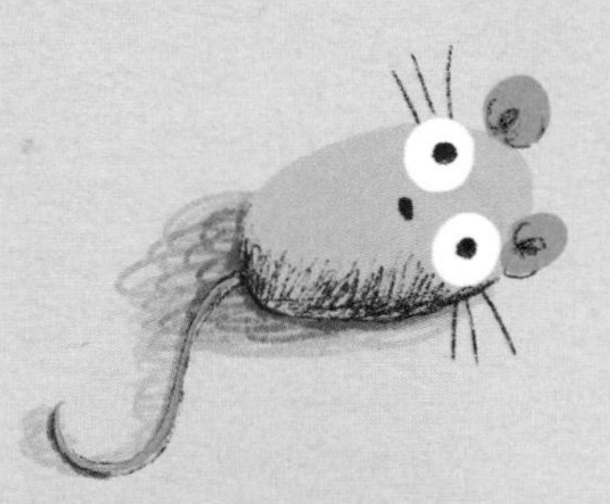

Sophie Blackall

 Nancy Paulsen Books

For our own Negative Cat, Claudia,
and Olive and Eggy,
who loved her.

Nancy Paulsen Books
An imprint of Penguin Random House LLC, New York

Visit us online at penguinrandomhouse.com

Library of Congress Cataloging-in-Publication Data
Names: Blackall, Sophie, author, illustrator.
Title: Negative cat / Sophie Blackall.
Description: New York: Nancy Paulsen Books, [2021] | Summary: "Max isn't a typical cat, but his loving owner still sees the best in him"—Provided by publisher.
Identifiers: LCCN 2021003128 |
ISBN 9780399257193 (hardcover) |
ISBN 9780698172982 (ebook) |
ISBN 9780698172999 (ebook)
Subjects: CYAC: Cats—Fiction. | Animals—Habits and behavior—Fiction. | Books and reading—Fiction. | Animal shelters—Fiction. | Human-animal relationships—Fiction.
Classification: LCC PZ7.B5319 Ne 2021 |
DDC [E]—dc23
LC record available at
https://lccn.loc.gov/2021003128

Manufactured in China
ISBN 9780399257193
10 9 8 7 6 5 4 3 2

Design by Marikka Tamura
Text set in KampFriendship
The illustrations in this book were created digitally and superimposed on the reverse side of vintage wallpaper salvaged from a falling-down house.

On Day 427 of asking for a cat…

CAT?
CAT?
THEY ALL SAW
A CAT
CAT?
MEOW

. . . my parents finally give in.

You have to feed it.
And clean out the litter.
It
better
not
have
fleas.

Also keep your room tidy!

And write to your grandma!

And read for twenty minutes every day!

Ugh! I'm not so great at reading! Words only make sense when I read them out loud slowly, and the kids at school stare and laugh at me. But I agree to the rules before my parents change their minds.

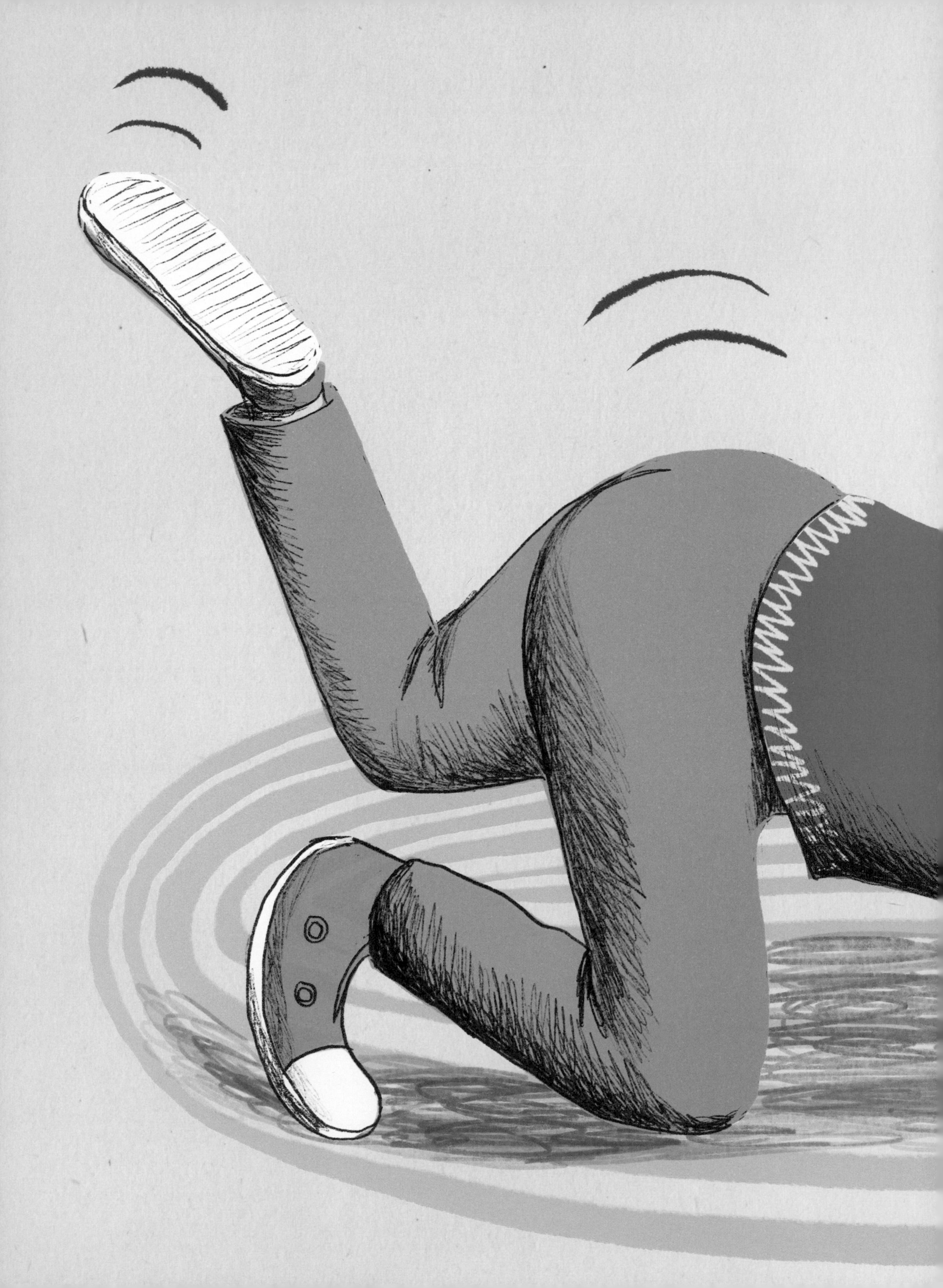

I'm getting a cat!

I'm getting a cat!

I'm getting a cat!

There are a million cats
in the rescue shelter,
and I want to take
them all home,
but Mom says,

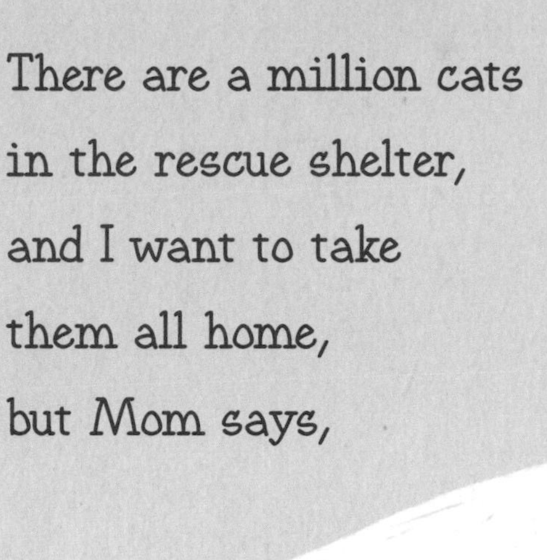

Then I find him.
The name on the cage
is Pookie, but that is
no name for this cat.
This cat is
Maximilian
Augustus
Xavier,
and we will call him
Max.

When we get home, I am excited to show Max his bed and his scratching post and his litter tray, and his scent-of-the-sea friskibits.

He is not excited.

The next day, I surprise Max with a toy mouse.

(He is not surprised.)

I tickle him with a feather.

(He is not ticklish.)

I tell him all my best jokes.

(He doesn't even smile.)

At school, my friends go on about how excellent their cats are.

Camilla can wear her cat like a scarf.

Jack's cat can fetch a stick.

Emilio's cat has its own Instagram.

My cat stares at the wall.

He's kind of negative, your cat.

On the weekend, Dad lets Max have the best parts of the paper.

Uncle Dave knits him a sweater.

Mom lets him borrow her shoes.

In return, Max leaves
hairballs on the rug,

his tail in the butter,

and poop in the vestibule.

He eats the flowers

and deletes my email to Grandma.

Everyone is
mad at Max.
He doesn't even purr.
I'm calling the shelter.
We should've gotten a dog.

And then they're mad at *me*.
YOUR ROOM IS A MESS!
HE HASN'T BEEN READING.
HAVE YOU EVEN WRITTEN TO GRANDMA?
I still love you, Max!

When the lady from the shelter comes,
Max and I hide in my room.
The grown-ups talk on and on.

Blah blah blah . . .

Commitment.

I have an idea. It's our only hope.

I tidy my room in record time.

I reach for a book...

I take a deep breath.

I begin to read slowly.

Out loud.

The only way

I know how.

Max stares, but he doesn't laugh.

I turn the page...

Max inches closer.
And closer.
And closer.

He tucks his head
under my arm.
I stay perfectly still
and read

and read . . .

. . . right to the very end of the book!

The lady from the shelter says Max and I should come and read to all the cats to cheer them up.

PRINCESS CHARLIE BEAR
LEFTY
Crackers
Lickerish
TAN HANDSOME
Margaret
REGINA
CUSTARD
LIEUTENANT GIBSON
Archie
DUDLEY
POCKET
Munjee

So we do. Now my whole class comes every Tuesday,
and we all read out loud, fast or slow,
however we like.
The cats are happy,
the lady at the shelter is happy,
and the parents are happy . . .

. . . sort of.
CAN WE PLEASE GET A CAT?
CAN WE PLEASE GET A CAT?
CAN WE

LEASE GET A CAT?
CAN WE PLEASE GET A CAT?
CAN WE PLEASE GET A CAT?
CAN WE PLEASE GET A CAT?
CAN WE PLEASE GET A CAT?

When my kids were little, we adopted a cat from an animal shelter. The sign on her cage said her name was Cinnamon, but we called her Claudia, after a character in *From the Mixed-Up Files of Mrs. Basil E. Frankweiler*. And because she had claws.

Over the years, she grew into what my son described as a Negative Cat. She ate the flowers, hogged the newspaper, and stared at the wall. She would ask to be stroked, then bite your hand. She would demand to be fed, throw up on the carpet, and then complain that she was hungry.

But we loved her.

A few years ago, I wrote a Negative Cat story but didn't know how to end it. I was about to put it away in the doomed file of unfinished stories when I read about something extraordinary happening at the Animal Rescue League of Berks County, Pennsylvania. Children who wanted to practice their reading were encouraged to read to cats! Not only were the cats nonjudgmental listeners, they became calmer and more sociable in the presence of readers. Children would read their books aloud, and before long, a cat would sidle up, lean against them, and purr. Sometimes a deep bond was formed, and a cat found its new home.

I would like to thank the Animal Rescue League of Berks County for their work supporting animal welfare and literacy, and the Heart of the Catskills Humane Society for allowing me to hang out with, draw, and read to their cats. The Animal Rescue League Book Buddies program has inspired similar programs across the country. You can contact your local shelter to see if they welcome readers or book donations.

Our own Claudia was a Negative Cat for most of her life, but she became surprisingly sweet in her final days. If only we'd read to her sooner.

—SOPHIE BLACKALL